IN DYING
STAR
LIGHT

PLANETFALL

EMILY McCOSH

BOOK 1

Published by Oceans In The Sky Press

OceansInTheSky.com

OCEANS IN
• THE SKY •

CHAPTERS

A bright, ice-cold planet blocks the light of its star. A chill settles over my old ship. I lean beside the controls and wait for permission to enter the atmosphere. Most planets don't have many regulations, but the smaller ones are often picky and paranoid. I can be patient. No one will deny me access.

"Did Audra give you any more leads?" Bat's voice is difficult and grunting, barely humanoid. Like me, he's a creature born of Amerov's cold and metal. It's the only constant place he's known besides the tiny halls of this ship.

Audra is my contact from Amerov who tipped me off on this job. She's been unusually quiet these past few months; I hadn't received a single word since the last job nearly half a year ago. Hearing from her was unexpected, especially considering she tipped me off on such a large bounty.

"Nothing new. She hasn't talked to me since."

When the comm beeps and I set the ship toward a docking station, Bat's big ears pop up from the tiny cot hung over the control panel. His snout appears over the edge as he gazes out the viewport.

"It looks cold."

I pulled up info on this spinning piece of space rock a few hours ago. "It's mostly snow and tundra. Gets some pretty bad storms, but apparently, this time of year is calm enough on this side of the planet."

Bat makes a disgruntled noise somewhere between a growl and a snarl and stuffs his head back into his blankets. He's a tough little thing, impossible to kill, but he doesn't like the freezing cold—not with all his hairless skin.

"I could find someone to knit you a sweater."

Two black eyes glare. With a round little face, squat snout, and each ear larger than my hand, it's a disconcerting image. Bat in a sweater would be a sight. Still, I'm going to pack some extra blankets into my pack if we leave the ship for any extended period of time.

Streaks of burning atmosphere surround the ship upon entry, irritating the heat sensors in my eyes until everything is a blur of red. If this bounty pays out, I'm going to find someone to replace the stupid things. Black market cyborg parts are difficult to get ahold of and not trustworthy, but it's better than returning to Amerov.

If I can get in touch with Audra after all this, maybe she'll know a reliable source.

Finally, the ship drops through, drifting in an arc through the clouds and toward the surface.

<*Welcome to Yayth. Population: 630,000.*> The comms read off an automated welcome from the approaching station. Only 630,000 humans in total. Not much to see here.

From this height, the south of the planet is visible, with entire continents of ice and snow where civilization hasn't spread. Commerce isn't high in such a place—the computer told me most settlements are either small farming communities or cities running huge fishing operations off the frigid oceans.

Space is cold, but not in the same way walking on this planet will be. Like Bat, I prefer the heat.

On the other hand, the sparse population means there aren't many hiding places for the bounty we're hunting. And the nastiness of the climate means they'll have to return to civilization eventually, even if they take off into the wilderness.

On a planet this small, a ship a little larger than mine

isn't impossible to hunt down.

Better yet, it's unlikely I'll run into any cyborgs out here. Not a single one.

I love jobs like this.

"You can come out if you want," I tell him. "The docking station is probably heated."

"Eh."

"And there's probably food."

"Let's go."

Bat drops from his cot onto my shoulder, then onto the floor, waddling to the bunk room on mechanical legs. Those contraptions are by far the most expensive things on my ship.

The docking station is a mess of ungainly metal protruding from the earth. Apparently, up here, there's ground beneath all the snow, not more ice—not that I can see it. Pristine white stretches in every direction. At least the air is clear, the sky a dark blue. A red star shimmers past the mist. No storms to block visibility or mess with the sensors on the ship.

The station perches on the bank of a choppy sea. Strange flat gray ships swarm the harbor and into the deep ocean. I don't know how they fish here, but sea vessels at their ports are emptying huge nets of sea life into holding tanks. There must be equipment on the undersides of the ships that performs the fishing. From this height, it's difficult to tell.

I'm the only space vessel in sight. And the hangar is small.

It should be real easy to find another ship out here.

Bat leaps onto the panel beside me, backpack clamped in his jaws. He drops it onto my hands, crawling inside. I'd call him a dog with a leash if he weren't smarter than most people.

This is the usual routine. It's easier to deter attention when he hides in the pack, and he isn't heavy.

"Spoiled," I tell him, petting the huge ears that earned him the nickname that stuck.

He gives a low growl.

The hangar is so small I ease the ship in manually, distrustful of the autopilot, careful not to ding the wingtips against the doors or the single other ship taking up space. Any larger and I'd be parking in the snow.

I don't need to pull up the bounty charts to know our neighbor ship isn't the one we're after. The bounty is for two people, and they're sharing an old junker a little larger and older than my own craft. The one beside us is small, shiny, brand-new, and solid white.

Because apparently there isn't enough white around this place.

A woman is operating a booth on the other end of the hangar. I try not to shiver as I head in her direction, Bat's nose sticking out of the pack, resting on my shoulder.

The lady takes one look at me through the glass and glances at the door as if she wants to bolt.

Wonderful. I should've put my hood up to begin with. Not everyone is skittish about cyborgs, but looking the way I do, people can tell something's incorrect. Most are tactful enough to avoid eye contact and get through the conversation as quickly as possible, which works fine for me.

I tug the fabric up over my hair until it shadows my face.

Her booth is sealed, but I can see her through the glass paneling. When she doesn't open it, I knock. The door slides open. A wash of heated air drifts over me, but I don't think she'd appreciate me stepping into her space.

"Do you keep logs of all the ships coming in and out?"

She squints. I can't imagine a more average, forgettable face. I suppose most people are a little forgettable when they don't have metal protruding from their bone structure.

"Um, yeah. It's in the control station where you got permission to land."

"Can I get access to that?"

Her eyes dart over me. I'm not wearing an Amerov uniform. I'm not wearing *any* uniform. Catching sight of Bat's snout over my shoulder, she turns a funny shade of pale.

"Bounty hunter?" she asks.

"Yep."

"You can, uh . . . You can ask. I'm not in charge of that kind of thing. In that door, two doors down to your left, then up a flight of stairs."

I follow the direction she points, feeling her eyes on me through the window, burning a hole in my back. Leaving the hangar takes us to the main market of the station, where workers ferrying goods in and out of stalls and the clatter of the massive ships outside make my hearing aids start up a faint buzzing sound. If it gets any louder, they're going to begin shrieking at me.

There's enough hustle and bustle that no one takes notice of a cyborg slipping in from the hangar, even if everyone here is remarkably human and unaltered. Enhancements are the cornerstone of Amerov, and those with plenty of money can pay for them. But they don't look like mine.

"I smell fish," Bat whispers.

"No kidding."

"Cooked fish."

He's right. The farther I walk in, it smells less like fresh and gutted sea life and more like fried and roasted meals. My mouth waters.

"After the flight logs."

"What if we piss someone off before then?"

"Don't piss anyone off."

"I meant *you*."

Sure, we've gone running from situations plenty of times. But it doesn't *always* happen. And he's just as bad as I am.

Two doors down behind vendor booths and workers of all shapes and sizes, I head up a stairwell. The whole building here is metal—I hop each step on my toes to keep from echoing too much. There's another sealed door, painted a lighter shade of gray than the metal walls, marked with *Records* in blocky letters. The metal sounds so flimsy when I knock that I'm certain I could tear through it like paper with my bare hands if the need arose.

Gotta love out-of-the-way backwater planets. Low tech and people who won't bother you.

A manual little peephole slides open, and the warm hum of a pistol flares to life against my forehead.

TWO

A pair of bored brown eyes stare at me from the other end of the gun.

Then they grow huge.

"What do you want?" he squeaks.

The hood only hides so much, and the stairwell is well lit. At least he doesn't appear twitchy with that weapon. My own pistol is in my belt, but this guy has a view of my hands. Bat slides farther into my pack.

"You just landed me in—"

"I know."

"I'd like to see the ship logs for the week. Anyone with a generation 5500 to 5600 ship."

He squints. "You from Amerov?"

"Yes," I say, because lying is easier, and most people

know the cyborg planet sometimes hires out their rogue creations. Plus, saying yes will probably put him more at ease, and comfortable people are easier to extract information from.

The gun disappears, the peephole sliding shut. For a moment, I wonder what I'll do if he barricades himself inside and calls the authorities. Then the door lock hisses out. My pulse returns to normal. *At least he didn't ask for my registration number.*

The control room is a squat little square space with a few control panels, some data storage boxes blinking blue lights along one wall, and a reclining chair that's probably seen more naps than actual recordings of flight logs.

"Sorry about the gun . . ." The controller is a twiglike young man with pale skin. Probably not much sunlight around here. "We get a lot of scavenger types looking to rip off smaller planets."

"It's fine," I say. "It probably wouldn't have killed me anyway."

If possible, he turns even paler.

Maybe that wasn't the most comforting thing I could've said.

"Er . . . what are you looking for, exactly?"

"Early generation 5500 ship, faded blue, two people—a brother and sister. Bounty chart said they were last sighted near here, and this is the only habitable planet for a while."

"Yeah, no, I remember that ship. Came in a few days ago. Weird people."

Bat shifts in the backpack.

"You talked to them?"

Gossip seems to relax him. "Sure. They wanted to know what's out west of here and where the next city is."

"What did you tell them?"

"This is the last major city until you reach the other side of the planet. Plenty of little settlements along the way, but not much else."

That works. "I still want to see their flight log. Do you track people at all?"

Flopping into his reclining chair, he unlocks his computer with his fingertips and taps away at the blinking keys. "We're not high-tech enough to track ships all across the planet. I can show you the path they took for the first few miles."

Better than most jobs I've had.

"What did they do, anyway?" he asks.

"Got too chatty with a cyborg."

"Yeah, I've heard that one before. You're not the only bounty hunter to have ever come through, you know."

I suppose others might have picked this small, corner-of-the-space-charts place to hide, so others of my kind might have passed through. I try not to shudder, especially not when it's warm enough in this stuffy little room for the gesture to be strange.

"Are there any on-planet?"

"Huh?"

"Cyborgs. Any others on-planet?"

He scrunches his face. "I haven't seen one in ages. A year maybe."

Probably not, then. I can't imagine a cyborg hanging out on an icebox like this for any longer than necessary. Amerov isn't warm, but the facilities are. Any conditioned Amerov number wouldn't hang around, and any rogue would probably pick a much warmer climate if they were trying to hunker down.

Some tension leaves my shoulders—not all, but the extra brought on by the idea of others of my kind in the same vicinity.

The kid finishes his search and leans back in his recliner. "Ta-da. Chart."

The computer isn't movable, so I'm forced to lean over him. I'm not in danger of making contact, but my skin still crawls. His breath brushes my face. No, that's not right. He isn't close enough. I'm imagining it.

I wonder if it's possible to hunt bounties without ever having to leave my ship.

Closeness seems to remind the kid he's frightened. I can feel him shifting away, though there isn't much space to move while he's seated. I straighten and back off a step.

"I'll take the file of this," I say. It's difficult to memorize the map with him breathing near me.

"I'm not . . . supposed to . . . give it to people . . ."

"I can stare at it, but you can't give me a copy?"

He opens and closes his mouth, then presses a few buttons and offers me a thread-thin cord. Plugging it into the port on the inside of my left arm gives me a small shock. If I were on Amerov, all my tech would have been upgraded ages ago—especially my eyes and ears.

"Thanks," I say, dropping the cord when it blinks. The kid's eyes flicker to my backpack. Bat's ears might be sticking up.

"Anything else I should know about heading west?"

"Um . . . don't land on the ice?" He sounds like he's asking.

"Why?"

"Big fish."

I can't tell if he's serious—the sweat along his forehead and jumpy twitches he's tapping along the floor with his foot would imply he is. I shouldn't have leaned so close to him. Maybe he got a good look at me under the hood. Doesn't matter. I don't plan on landing on the ice.

I want to ask him if I'll be followed, but I suspect he'd lie. Lots of people say whatever they think won't make me angry.

Which, ironically, ticks me off.

Anyway, this place doesn't have the manpower to be following slightly suspicious cyborgs. They can't even track outside a few miles.

Trying not to make further eye contact, I slip back out the door. The icy stairwell is welcome despite the chill it drags down my spine. Rather the cold than a warm cramped space with some human.

"Someone's never seen an unregistered before," Bat grumbles, crawling out of the pack to perch halfway on my shoulder. "Did you get a look at the map before you downloaded it?"

"A little. Was mostly just a straight flight northwestish of here. I can get the exact direction when I plug it into the ship."

"That's not going to take us very far."

"I know."

We don't have much to go on. Just the sparseness of the planet and the assurance there are only a few large cities the fugitives might be traveling to. They have a ship built for traversing between stars, but it isn't a deep-space craft meant to be self-sustainable for weeks and weeks without touching civilization. They'll need to stock up on food and fuel eventually.

And now we have a direction.

THREE

Bat smacks his jaws around some sort of fried fish. The whole eatery smells of oil, salt, and brine, but the food is decent. I haven't had anything so rich and greasy in ages. I only make it halfway through my meal before picking at the flaky meat with my fork, full.

"Are you happy now?" I ask.

Bat stops smacking long enough to give me a cool stare. Two women a few tables away have been staring for the last ten minutes, enough I'm getting jittery. I scoop Bat off the table and head for the exit—he can eat in the ship. There's nothing else helpful here. We're already stocked on weeks of food and water, and I fueled up at the last planet we passed. Everything's expensive here anyway. There's a reason we need this bounty.

Far to my left, the giant doors to the fishery open with the crack of built-up ice. Frost gusts in, not hitting us through all the booths. There's a vague shuffling in the direction of the doors, but most everyone stays where they are. Bat flattens his giant ears at all the noise. Slipping back into the hangar brings the real cold. I pick up my pace.

Someone's lingering near my ship's airlock.

Bat goes rigid. I set him on the ground. The man sitting on the gangplank up to the airlock watches him scurry around the other side of the ship. Bat can get in a smaller hatch on the opposite side of the ship I can't squeeze through, or the one on the top. He can also point the ship's gun at the stranger should the need arise.

At least the man is human. There's a weight off.

"Nice ship," he says.

I glance at the rust bucket, which is barely worthy of flying out of atmosphere, then back at whoever this idiot is who thinks he's clever. It's been a long day—but it's barely midmorning.

"Go away." Sometimes having zero manners throws people off into actually listening.

"I want to see your registration number," he says, standing, hands behind his back like he's comfortable. There's nothing impressive about him: tan skin as if he's spent plenty of time in the reflected sun of this ice planet, or maybe relocated from somewhere with a better climate; clothes a dirty red color, the cut of them resembling a uniform. Maybe an official? For whatever such is worth in a place like this.

The uniform doesn't appear warm enough for subzero temps.

"No," I say, then go to step past him.

He steps in front of me. I glance at his boots. Soft toed. Easy to stomp on with the sharp heel of my own boots.

"I said I would like to see your registration number, cyborg."

His expression is so passive I could almost think him some sort of robot. But he isn't. I can feel the heat coming off his skin and smell sour breath, even when it's a puff of frost in the cold.

"I'd personally like to not get into a fight with you, whoever you are," I say, then get the satisfaction of his eyebrows bunching in annoyance.

"I run security for this sector, and apparently, you intimidated my records official into giving you a map."

Calling that boy in the stuffy room an "official" of any kind is almost funny enough to make me smile.

"I didn't intimidate. I asked. Try looking for officials with a little more spine if that bothers you."

"I want your—"

"I don't care. I'm not obligated to give it to you. Now, would you like to move, or shall I move you?"

Behind him, the ship hums to life. He starts a little, which would've also been funny if he hadn't jumped a little *closer* to me. I lock my muscles to keep from backing up. I look much, *much* more frightening than he does— than anyone, really, even with my hood up. It's something I need to remember. It would be heaps easier if people didn't believe they could get up close and personal with cyborgs just because most are programmed by Amerov to be nice and mechanical. Well, not *nice*, but stable enough they won't fly into a rage because someone annoys them.

Everyone's either getting as far from me as possible or right up in my face. At least this idiot is sweating. It's freezing to his hairline.

"Amerov regulations say any planet official can request—"

"Good thing for me I'm not part of Amerov's regulations."

"What the hell does that mean?"

"If you think *really* hard, it might come to you."

He gives me a once-over. I don't have a uniform, though not every Amerov number has a uniform. Given my hood and gloves, he probably only knows I'm a cyborg because the kid I got the map from told him, or maybe he can see the spare wires or ports visible on my neck or behind my ears. The metal running down my jawbone might be visible.

Finally, slowly, he says, "You're unregistered."

When I was a teenager, the word would've bothered me. These days, it's kinda funny. "There ya go."

He does a weird twitching motion like he wants to back off, but his pride is getting in the way. I can deal with getting close to him for a second.

Pulling back my hood, I lean forward and say, "Move."

He steps sideways. Good. I didn't want to touch him.

Stomping up the walkway, I mutter, "Go have a power trip on someone else."

The airlock cycling closed is a comforting hiss.

"I wanted to shoot him," Bat says from the control panel. He still has his fish in one metal paw.

"Maybe next time."

The engines are still warm and getting hotter, so it isn't taking long for the cabin to fill with heat. I shrug off my coat, throw my gloves aside, and flop into the pilot's seat. Out the viewport, I watch the human hovering around the hangar. He doesn't even appear armed. What an idiot. Probably wanted a cut of the bounty. Wouldn't be the first time.

I hover the ship out the hangar in case he decides to have the main door sealed.

Pulling a cord from a cubbyhole in the control panel, I plug it into my arm and transfer the map. The little panel near my wrist stores money and any private files I need. One good thing about being unregistered: I don't actually have any private files someone might want to steal. Just money, even if it's running low.

The panel in my arm is nothing like the chip in the back of most cyborgs' necks. I have the port there, along with all the other metal and wiring, but it's empty.

Flicking through the shimmering blue hologram of the map, I realize I could've left without it. It's merely a wavering red line pointing northwest of here. The map itself isn't even large enough to cover much outside this city. I have maps leaps and bounds more detailed already downloaded into my ship's computer.

At least it's a direction.

And I'm here earlier than any Amerov cyborgs that may be sent after this bounty.

"Aaron," Bat says as the comm starts up a soft beeping.

It isn't the alarm of someone trying to contact me—a small blessing—but of something big coming our way. A swirling mass of blue shows up on the thermal map. Popping the hatch on the top of the ship, I stick my head out long enough to see the massive wall of a storm heading our direction. The dark clouds are nearly solid, with a hint of lightning here and there. Sea ships are turning back to port. The giant door to the marketplace seals.

It probably won't hurt our ship, but it'll make finding

another vessel a pain.

Any other hunter could show up if the storm causes a large enough delay.

Anyone from Amerov.

"You're letting in the cold!" Bat claws at my pant leg.

I seal the hatch. Waiting it out won't do us any good.

"Let's go," I say, flipping the autopilot off and blasting the ship over the icy wasteland, following the little red line of our bounty.

FOUR

The planet has become pillars of ice by the time the storm catches us.

I watch it on the ship's thermal map instead of the plains of white out the front viewport. My eyes don't appreciate extremes in temperature. Heat confuses them, and a never-ending frigid cold will just make them glitch. I lost the ability ages ago to switch to my normal vision at will, so they filter back and forth of their own accord, often giving me a headache. By the time the monster weather blocks out everything on the radar behind us, I'm ready to admit defeat and start scouting out the landscape for a good place to hunker down.

At least no one else will be heading out in this weather, Amerov or otherwise. I've been checking the ship's temperature sensors, and no one's followed us.

Bat is staring out the viewport from over the edge of his cot. His ears are plastered back. Sure, he hates the cold, but this storm looks like it could tear apart the only ship he's ever called home. I didn't expect it to be this quick or severe. I wouldn't've tried to outrun it.

"I've landed this thing in worse storms. We'll just find a place to wait it out."

"I know," he says, but tension still knots the thick muscles of his back.

I don't know how to further reassure him. He gets nervous easily, and it's not as if I'm any better.

Wind rattles the ship. Snow swirls in and around the engines. Ice gathers at the corners of the windows. The heat of the engine is quite enough to keep out the cold of any planet. It's made to withstand the never-ending nothing of space.

Still, I don't appreciate the worsening visibility. The ship's radar is only good for different temperature changes. It doesn't help when there are pillars of ice shooting into the sky the same temperature as the surrounding planet. Even the red sun is long blocked from view. Only a handful of settlements have dotted the way, all too small to have hangars capable of containing a vessel even as large as the one we're tracking. All too small for us.

There. I lean over the controls to get a better look

out the viewport. The radar isn't giving me anything. Definitely a house.

Built right into the ice of a pillar.

Well, that's a new one.

I hover the ship lower, circling the pillar. The computer begins beeping at me about the cold. I shut off the alarm. If it's going to get colder, visibility will definitely be gone.

Computer files said storms aren't supposed to roll in this time of year. Figures.

"We're not landing near people, are we?" Bat hops down to the controls, dragging a blanket with him.

"The ice looks solid, and they have a hangar. We'll just land in. They probably won't realize we're here. Visibility's bad, and the storm is louder than the engine."

I wonder how much swirling ice will overload the engines, or if such a phenomenon is possible. There aren't unavoidable ice storms in space.

Circling the ship around the pillar where it's least likely anyone in the home might see, I take our ship down along the icy ground. I'm surprised I managed to see the home. A plain stone wall is all that differentiates it from the ice, and even the gray rock is beginning to blend in as flying slush pelts it. Up close, there's no sign of life, save the faintest glow of light from the cracks in one of the shuttered windows.

What do people even *do* out here?

The hangar door is open. It may not even close. Though small, it's large compared to most around here. A hovercraft is parked near a much larger ship covered in tarps. I slide our vessel in close and kill the engine before anyone can hear. With its lull gone, there's just the storm wind tearing at the tundra and howling against the open hangar door. Ice splatters the metal hull. I wonder how long the heat will last with the engine off. I'd rather not fire it back up and let anyone know we've taken refuge. I doubt the locals are hostile, but I don't want to interact.

We're already going to haul the two prisoners back to Clock—the highest-security prison the cold depths of space have to offer—in our tiny ship. That much human contact is going to be plenty.

At least there are 300,000 credits in it for us.

For a while, I watch the cold of the storm swirl in shades of blue along the temperature map, then eventually wander away. If we were out in space, I'd settle into something—a puzzle or music or some sort of mindless exercise—but here on a foreign planet parked in an unfamiliar hangar, I'd rather not put my thoughts elsewhere.

Leaning against the round port window along the left of the ship, I attempt a better look at the other vessel under all the tarps. Something that size should be pretty expensive. I don't know if living out in this wasteland in a house built into ice and stone means you have little money or more than you know what to do with.

I squint at the ship. It's mostly concealed under all the plastic and the ice building along the glass of my round window. It looks to be a fairly early 5500-century ship, much like mine. Difficult to tell what kind of shape it's in.

A little bigger than ours.

Blue. The wing is a faded blue.

"No way," I mutter.

I'm tempted to pop the hatch and slide out for a better look, but the heat in here is already fading. Even when I kill the engine out in space, it takes days for the inside to get cold and the life support to begin sending me alerts.

How is it already so cold?

Bat clinks over on his metal paws, leaping onto the ledge of the window. Pressing his snout to the glass, he shivers. I check the temperature manually on the controls so I don't have to fire up the computer. Well below freezing. Already.

It's been fifteen minutes.

Nothing in the info about the planet said it gets so cold so fast, especially not at this time of year. The kid in the control room didn't mention anything about the weather—just to stay off the ocean ice.

I need to fire the engine back up to keep us warm. Fantastic.

"Is that the bounties' ship?" Bat asks. "It can't be."

"Looks like it."

"Do you think they know the people living here?"

"Maybe. Maybe they got caught in the storm like us. It isn't supposed to be this cold."

I kick the main engine back to life. It sputters and shuts off. Not for the first time.

"Piece of crap," I mutter.

I try again. This time it doesn't even spit and moan to fake me out. There isn't a single noise. The next few tries yield the same results.

Well, that's new.

"What is it?"

I pull the paneling up in the center of the floor. "I don't know. Maybe it's the cold."

The pocket under the floor is so unexpectedly frigid that the fleshy parts of my fingers stick to the metal, peeling away painfully when I yank back.

"Don't touch the metal with your skin."

All of Bat's legs are completely mechanical, so it shouldn't be a problem.

Thankfully, the melon-sized crystal shimmering blue in the center of the engine appears perfectly in shape. Everything else is easier to replace than the rare resource, which keeps deep-space vessels traveling at top speed.

Bat hops down at my feet, scuttling into the little

spaces under the primary engine where I can't reach without taking the whole thing apart.

Faintly, something outside thumps. The hair along the back of my neck rises. I've always thought it's a little funny I'm still human enough for that reaction. Silently, I hop out of the compartment and take a look out the wide front window.

"Aaron, there's lots of ice down here . . ." Bat mutters. "Hold on."

There isn't much to see, just the swirling of the storm and the tarp on the other ship flapping in the wind. I don't want to pop the hatch until we can get the engine back up.

A fist slams against the airlock.

FIVE

I go still. I can't believe anyone's out in such bitter cold when even *my* fingers are going numb and I can see my breath in my own ship. Bat pops back into view, pitch-black eyes and huge ears visible over the edge of the engine.

More knocking.

I snatch the pistol off the wall, pull my hood up, and crack the airlock. It hisses out pressure but takes a great deal of shoving and swearing to get open. Ice has coated the wall, nearly sealing the door to the rest of the ship. If most of my muscles weren't synthetic, I might not have gotten it open. A wash of the biting cold clings to my skin. Despite my best efforts, I shudder, grinding my teeth so they don't chatter.

The man standing below me has the right idea. I can't see much of him save his eyes with the layers of fabric wrapped around him. He edges his scarf down, bushy beard beginning to collect ice. A rifle is tucked under his arm, but its model is old enough I'm surprised it works. It might even have old-fashioned bullets.

Not a rich family, then.

He blinks and, to his credit, appears more surprised than alarmed. Probably because he can't see most of me.

In a foreign, difficult-to-catch accent, he asks, "You a cyborg?"

Slowly, I nod. I'm not wearing gloves, so it's pretty obvious, and he can probably see the shadows of metal ports and wires in my face and neck.

"Wow. I've never met one before."

"Glad to impress you."

He cocks his head. Sarcasm isn't programmed into Amerov's soldiers, so I should probably learn not to fire it off whenever I'm uncomfortable.

"You from Amerov?"

How should I answer? Saying yes would be a blatant lie. This man might not know anything about Amerov, but if he does, he'll know I'm lying. Saying no is bound to frighten him. He isn't some planet official. If people are nervous about the outwardly pleasant and emotionless Amerov numbers, they're downright terrified of the "rogue cyborgs" roaming the galaxy.

"Sort of," I say, hoping he'll get the picture.

He grunts, gives me a once-over, and nods, which I suppose means he does.

"Well, you'd better come in, then."

"What?"

"These storms are too cold to live in, even in a ship. You'll freeze."

Why does he care? I suppose some people are simply *nice*—even to cyborgs who are obviously incorrect. Weird. But the last place I want to be is stuck in the house of some strange family.

"I'm fine," I say, beginning to ease the airlock shut before I start shivering too hard. "Just getting my engine started back up."

"It won't start."

I pause. "What?"

"Yeah. I know it sounds weird, but these storms shut down engines all the time. No one can fly in them. It freezes them right through unless you've got special equipment. It'll be fine once the storm passes, but you won't be starting it up until then."

I glance at Bat, who's listening in, eyes wide. It seems too strange a thing for the man to make up.

"How cold does it get? The files on this planet didn't mention that."

"Yeah, we're a bit of an off-the-star-charts place—I bet the info isn't good. A good three hundred degrees below, I'd say. We don't measure exactly, just stay inside. The ice tends to . . . grow on things."

Well.

Damn.

I didn't know that was possible.

The man stares expectantly, bouncing to keep warm even in his special clothing. Again, I glance at Bat. Shivering. Waiting for me to make a decision. Most of my body is synthetic, so I'd probably survive cold that bad, even if I lost most of the human skin on my limbs in the process. Though highly enhanced, Bat's mostly all organic save his limbs.

"All right," I mutter. "I have a friend with me. He looks like an animal, but he isn't. If you try to harm him, you won't like what I'll do."

He shrugs, unbothered. "Follow me."

I nod and then, because most people aren't this nice, say, "Thanks."

I wrap Bat in a blanket, ignoring his struggling; hiding his appearance will make this less strained. Tucking both pistols into the straps on my leg and belt, I grab the pack Bat was hiding in earlier. With the ship out of commission, there isn't much I need from it now that I'm armed.

Ice coats the hangar floor. I manage not to slip as I shove the airlock closed behind me and follow the man toward a door on the opposite wall, one arm holding Bat, other hand on my gun.

Never trust people who are too nice.

"Is that ship yours?" I ask, nodding at the blue one under the tarps.

"Nah, we've got a visitor. Wanted shelter from the storm, same as you. They didn't try to stay in their ship though," he adds with a laugh, heaving open the heavy door leading into his house.

They. More than one of them. A brother and a sister maybe. I wonder if they'll panic the moment they see a cyborg.

This could get interesting.

I've never enjoyed a blast of heat more than when I step into the man's house. He shoves the heavy door shut with a grunt, eyeing Bat but not appearing too alarmed, leaning his rifle against the wall. Not too bright, this one. I suppose he makes up for it with kindness. So far. It must have paid off for him at some point—being so kind. I don't let myself scowl.

The house is too dark to see much. It's a square main room, not tall, with doors off to the left that must lead farther into the pillar of ice. A few windows on my right face the storm, but they're shuttered tight with metal paneling. A hot red fire burns in a hearth. They're actually heating this place with fire. How old-fashioned. I can't believe they have anything to burn out here. Perhaps it's fuel. Some sort of spice I can't identify hangs in the air, and I'm unsure if it's the flames or something else.

Two children peek out a door. Even in the dim light, I see both their mouths pop open. Great. *What do I look like to them in the dark?* I've had enough experiences with children screaming and pointing that they make me jumpy. At least these two just stare.

"Who's this?"

A woman appears from the room as well, twitches, and then pats her wrinkled pants in a nervous gesture. All I can see in the dark is her short stature and midlength hair. My eyes are only giving me blobs of heat, which are about as unhelpful as they could possibly be.

"Another one lost in the storm," the man says, shrugging out of all his gear.

There's a painful silence.

"Do you get a lot of stragglers out here?" I ask. Small talk is good. Small talk makes humans comfortable. It doesn't do much for me, but if they're comfortable, I don't have to feel so much like I want to find a crack in the ice and fling myself into it.

"Oh, lots," the woman says in the same uncomfortable voice. "We're thinking of building another bedroom."

I can't tell if she's serious or attempting a joke, so I just nod. She probably can't see my expression very well anyway.

"Another idiot like us, huh?" says a male voice from one of the chairs near the fire. Two more faces appear. They're close to the firelight, and their expressions drop at the sight of me.

A man and a woman. Brother and sister.

I recognize their faces from the bounty charts.

SIX

Bat's ears flatten. No one should see him in the dark. Hopefully the silent seconds that follow aren't as tense for everyone else as they are for me. I work on unknotting the muscles in my shoulders.

Finally, the brother says, "Wow, a cyborg. Haven't seen one of you in a while."

Not since your sister broke out of Clock? I think but don't say

One would think such a reputation would make for dangerous people—breaking out of the highest-security prison in the galaxy *after* breaking into Amerov—but all the information in the bounty charts leads to both of them being pretty passive. The woman wasn't violent with the prison guards, and the only sign of violence elsewhere is one assault against an Amerov number who arrested her. Nothing from the brother. I don't know why they broke into an Amerov facility (and don't particularly care), but I would've punched the number too, so I can't fault her for that.

If I didn't want their bounties, I'd probably get a kick out of it.

Sunken into chairs beside the fireplace, neither appears dangerous. They have weapons—I'm certain of it—but haven't drawn them.

Not everyone's as touchy as I am.

But they must know they're being tracked. Most cyborgs aren't bounty hunters—not even all unregistered numbers get into this line of work—but one of my kind out here has to set off alarms. If they're panicking, they aren't letting it show. In the firelight, I glimpse nothing but vague curiosity. The male looks a little amused . . . if I'm reading his expression correctly.

The female is looking at Bat. I've never been more grateful for the darkness. Between my hood and the blanket covering Bat, we shouldn't look too frightening. I'd rather no one know I'm after the siblings until the storm passes. Getting in a fight here and now, trapped in this house with the deadly cold outside, would be a rookie move—plus, I'd rather not hurt the locals who were nice enough to invite me in only to find themselves between a rogue bounty hunter and his target.

A table and chairs sit by the shuttered windows overlooking the kitchen counter, and I slide into the farthest seat. It's warm enough over here. This way I don't have to take off my hood.

The siblings fall into some sort of conversation, foreheads close, muttering words my hearing aids can't catch. From this angle, I see their weapons: a pistol on the coffee table at their feet and another on the brother's leg, strapped to his thigh like mine. The sister wears a lot of clothing, loose and baggy in fit, and I wouldn't be surprised if she's carrying a few other things in there. From the way he keeps glancing over her shoulder at me, I figure at least the brother is suspicious.

Bat squirms in my lap, falling still under his blanket when the man who invited us in comes close enough to rummage around the kitchen cupboards. His wife is tending to the fire. The children are nowhere to be seen, but I have a difficult time believing they'd head to bed with a cyborg in the house. Poor planets don't get things like us. We're the soldiers and guards and weapons of the galaxy. The private protection of the royal family (the fact they're *royals* even though they run a democracy has always been a tad hilarious) and often hired out by those with enough money to pay for them.

Unless there's a catastrophic event, I wouldn't be

surprised if this planet's never had a single visitor like me. Well, a single Amerov cyborg. I'm somewhere in between—not that these folks need to know. The kid back at the station *did* say I'm not the first.

"Are you looking for someone?" The man's voice makes me jump.

I glance at him. He's still rummaging through the cupboard, the ice having melted out of his beard. He has a pleasant, open way to his expression. But I've met such people before. My fingers ache around their metal components.

"What gave it away?" I say, then realize it's not helpful to be snippy. "Yes, I'm looking for someone."

I have the siblings' full attention now.

"Bounty hunter?"

"Yes."

"I heard a lot of cyborgs go into bounty hunting. At least when they . . . er, I mean, at least when they don't stay with Amerov."

"The word you're looking for is *unregistered*," I say blandly, and the man tucks his chin like he wants to hide his mouth in his beard.

Unregistered and *rogue* are the two common phrases for Amerov numbers who desert the planet that created them, for those who endure all the programming and physical changes but can't handle it. There aren't many, but the danger they pose makes the myths widespread. Usually, something malfunctions or breaks with their programming chip, and a cyborg body with a broken chip (and human mind) is a horrifying combination.

I can't exactly count myself in with those creatures when I never received my chip in the first place. But it's a good enough word, and that little bit of information is a secret I'll take to my grave. Only Bat knows.

And Audra. My stomach churns.

"Is it a big bounty?" the man asks.

He sounds eager in an unalarming sort of way. They're a poor family. Even a small bounty would have them drooling. It isn't the same as the aggressive moron who tried to stop me at the station. If all goes well, I might cut them in on it just a little—it's a huge bounty, after all, and a little must go a long way out here. They've been kind. We'll see how the rest of this storm goes. In the meantime, I don't want them to know.

"Not much," I say, scraping to come up with one of the smaller bounties the charts listed in this area in case the siblings have been keeping an eye on them. "Some small-time thief. There aren't many planets out here where he could have stocked up on supplies. Wouldn't have been worth it if I weren't flying by."

The man deflates. "Oh."

Near the fire, the brother's expression loses some of

its alarm. The sister still watches me over her shoulder. I try to remember their names from the bounty sheet—my tablet is still tucked into my pack, and I don't want any of them seeing me scrolling through it.

The silence stretches again, and I actually think I like it less than the talking.

"What do you do out here? This place looks pretty barren."

"Fishing." The man offers a glass of something, and I wave it off. "This whole place is built on ice. It's dozens of feet thick and never melts, but there's a huge ocean underneath. The catch here is expensive. We drill through the ice."

I look at the stone floor. Dozens of feet of ice beneath us. Then an unending ocean. After living most my life drifting in the space between dying starlight, I'd think my stomach wouldn't twist so much at the idea.

Didn't that kid at the station say never to land on the ice?

The brother leans over the back of his chair and asks, "What could you possibly be fishing?"

A rumble shakes the house. I'm standing in a second. So are the siblings. Above us, I can hear the ice moan and sway. *Is it cracking?* Bat crawls from his blanket to perch on my shoulder with sharp claws.

The man snorts.

At least I'm not the only one who stares at him in shock.

He jabs his thumb at the window, out toward the expanse of ice. "We're fishing for that."

SEVEN

"**S**orry, what?" the brother asks.

The shuddering fades, replaced by the sudden and unnerving awareness of a giant creature slithering hundreds of feet below us, scraping its back along the ice. My pulse thuds behind my ears.

"It's a gengen," the man says, entirely too cheerful.

"You can't just say that like it explains anything," the sister says.

The man rolls his eyes. "Sit back down. It's a giant fish. Very rare, very valuable. We catch maybe one a year, and that's enough to live off of. Two if the stars are smiling on us."

I sit, mainly because I don't want them thinking I'm rattled. Bat drops back into my lap, but the wife is already staring at him with wide alarmed eyes. At least she doesn't scream.

"How big is *giant*?" the brother asks, sitting slower, eyeballing the floor as if it might crack at any moment.

The man squints, thoughtful. "You know your ship out there? Like four, maybe five of those lined up wing to wing."

The siblings exchange glances. The brother says, "You know, most planets just have different insects, not giant monster fish from the pits of hell."

That isn't true, but I get the point. Most settled planets don't have such drastically different and dangerous species. Though I know of a few where those "different insects" will kill. Less hospitable planets often have terrible monsters to go along with their uninhabitable atmospheres.

"How big is the drill?" I ask.

"Huh?"

"The drill. To get through the ice. How big is it?"

The man shrugs. "Fifteen feet across."

"I didn't see anything that big outside."

"Store it in the other side of the house."

I'm assuming he means the other side of the giant ice pillar.

"How tall is it?"

Another shrug. "Not as tall as you'd think. It drills

down and cracks the ice the rest of the way."

"How do you get to the fish?"

He eyes me, then sits on the opposite side of the table like he's thrilled someone's taking an interest. "They tend to come to the surface in the dawn or twilight. Not often. But we have equipment that can tell if they're close. They're very territorial. You crack the ice and show them the sunlight, and they'll launch themselves right out of the water to eat whatever's bothering them."

"And you live right above them?" the brother asks.

"They can't tell we're here unless we bother the ice. One time one of the ice pillars toppled over. Made 'em mad. Two huge ones tried to attack the broken ice. They don't mind us just walking around or using the hovercraft."

Bat gives me a look from under the table as if he doubts it.

The children are watching from the doorway of their room again. I've pushed my luck enough with these people not becoming hostile, so I don't give them a wave, just stare in return. The smaller one—a girl of maybe ten—wanders out to stand behind her father. He ruffles her hair tenderly. I stare at the floor. Anywhere other than at them.

"Are you a real cyborg?" the little girl asks.

The father chokes on his drink.

Real? Funny way to put it. Even with my hood up, I suppose the child can tell.

"Real how?" I ask.

The girl shrugs. Much like the others, all I can see is her outline and the length of her hair—a blob of heat in my malfunctioning eyes.

So I shrug too.

Silence stretches back out. The girl half bends sideways as if she's trying to look under the table at Bat without me noticing. Bat hisses. Everyone jumps. I rub his ear. No use scaring the crap out of all the humans before the storm passes.

Which reminds me. "How long do these storms last?"

"Few hours to a few days. This one isn't all that bad. Probably a few hours."

Not all that bad? My ship won't even start.

Still, some tension leaves my shoulders. Hours. Days would have been so much worse.

Both parents herd their kids to their bedroom. The quiet is nice now that no one's staring at me. The fire crackles, and the storm howls. This place must have feet upon feet of ship insulation to keep out the cold and sound so well. The siblings are in their own little world by the fire, though the brother has the good sense to keep glancing my way.

Zane. That's the brother's name. The sister's name starts

with *L*, I think, but it wasn't a name I'd heard before. Their last name is still rattling around somewhere in the back of my head where I can't call it to mind.

The father is still shuffling around, but the mother seems to be gone with the children. No one speaks to me or seems expectant for me to speak to them, so I lean back in the wooden chair and try to find something to think about. As discretely as possible, I ease my tablet from the pocket of my pack and send the feed to flicker through my glass eyes. They're not much good for such things anymore, but so long as there aren't any drastic changes in temperature, the stupid contraptions can manage to overlay the translucent words atop the rest of the room without them being disrupted by blobs of heat.

Bounties out in this sector are pretty pathetic, the two siblings across the room being the glaring exception. Lalia. That's the sister's name. Zane and Lalia DeLouve. He's thirty-four (same as me, which is interesting), and she's thirty-eight, and both have a pretty minor record not much worse than mine—minor theft of things unspecified, a few incidences of taking their ship through a populated space they weren't supposed to (I've done so once or twice myself), and then the one glaring exception.

Both broke into Amerov.

I physically can't imagine it.

To be fair, I can't imagine why anyone would go to

Amerov, even the thousands of people who volunteer for the "upgrades." But breaking in? Maybe I'll ask them what they could have possibly wanted on that barren rock. Maybe. Once they're secured in my ship.

The sister was caught and delivered to Clock. She broke out with the help of her brother. And now they're on the run.

I kill the feed and stare at the back of the sister's head. Neither looks like the type who could perform a break-in at one of Amerov's many facilities as well as a *breakout* at one of the highest-security prisons to ever exist.

Maybe it's the dark room around us and all the isolation of this planet, but I'm suddenly hopeful I haven't bitten off more than I can chew. I never have in one of my jobs.

Well, I've lived through all my jobs at least.

•

A pounding on the door startles me upright.

I wasn't dozing, but I wasn't paying attention either. The hours blurred in the long night until I was slumping in the chair, gazing at some spot on the floor, listening to the father snore where he'd fallen asleep in a recliner opposite the siblings.

From the way all three of them jump, I'd guess they were all asleep.

The father grabs his rifle.

Someone out in this storm? I glance at the windows. It's still raging but has calmed enough that most of the noise isn't making it past the walls. Either the person knocking got lost on foot and is near dead, or the chill has broken enough for ships to be back up and running.

Glancing at the siblings, I put my hand on my pistol under the table.

Bat digs his claws into my leg, then jumps to the floor and slithers off, hidden in shadows along the far wall.

"Expecting anyone?" I ask the fisherman.

"No."

He slides open a book-sized metal sheet on the door I hadn't noticed. Haven't seen one of those in a while, just on the control room door back at the station. Even from here, the frost from the open hatch crawls across my skin.

Leaning his face against the peephole, the fisherman slouches his head sideways, exasperated. He yanks the door open and drags the man in, shoving it tight again and setting aside his rifle.

"What do you want, Guli?"

I recognize the dirty red color of the man's uniform—now in the form of a thicker winter coat and pants—without needing to see his face. He's the idiot who stopped me in the hangar, trying to get in on my bounty. I barely manage not to roll my eyes.

Then I *really* hope he doesn't notice me lingering in the shadows.

"Heard there's a bounty hiding out around this area. Thought I'd check it out."

Heat rises in my chest. No way he followed me out here—I was checking. And it's been *hours.*

"You're not a bounty hunter," the fisherman says with enough amusement in his voice that it's almost funny how visibly Guli bristles.

Even with my limited information, I'd tend to agree.

"As much as anyone else," Guli snaps, which I doubt, and it seems he's trying real hard to be in control of the situation.

Can I slip into one of the rooms without him noticing?

"Looking for the thief too?" the fisherman asks, and I regret even letting him know I'm a bounty hunter.

"Thief? No. Couple of escaped Clock convicts. There was an Amerov cyborg at the station this morning looking for the direction they'd headed."

Well.

How wonderful.

For a moment, the fisherman goes quiet. He looks at me, and so does Guli. Then at the siblings. Following his eyes, I see them both frozen in their chairs. The brother's eyes catch mine.

Then everyone draws their guns.

EIGHT

I dive under the table. The weasel from the station has the good sense to hit the ground as well. Both siblings take a shot at him.

Going for the easier target, I see.

Shame they miss.

I take aim at the brother's gun and squeeze the trigger. He doesn't look nearly as surprised or freaked as I'd hoped when it flies from his hand in a shower of sparks. The sister spins on me, expression grim. *Reluctant?*

From the shadows of the room, Bat disarms her in much the same way. She gasps, shaking her hand, whipping around as she searches for him in the darkness. From the other room, there's a good deal of shrieking.

Right. The kids.

Guli's getting to his feet, ice-coated hair sticking every which way, eyes huge. The fisherman has his rifle, head swiveling from Guli to the siblings to me sliding out from under the table. No one's going after him, and he can tell.

Guli aims his pistol at me, and I almost, *almost*, laugh. He thinks he's going to take me out with that little thing? When I was only a child on Amerov, Audra told me I was too old for a pebble shooter like that. I point my pistol—a useful weapon, thank you very much—and the man takes one look at the dimly glowing blue muzzle and lowers his own to the floor. I guess he isn't *entirely* an idiot.

Until his eyes flicker to the siblings.

"Don't," I tell him. Because I'm not into killing people, especially not humans who aren't smart enough to know what's good for them. I could shoot him in the arm or leg, sure, but then I'd have a mess to clean up. And he's so close to the fisherman that I don't want to play target practice with the pistol in his hand and hit the innocent behind him. No one's a perfect shot.

He doesn't listen, raising his arm in their direction, opening his mouth as if he's going to give some order no one would listen to.

The brother tackles him.

Lowering my gun, I watch the scuffle on the kitchen

floor. *Who tackles someone with a gun?* From the corner of my eye, I watch the sister trying to creep sideways, only to stop dead when Bat growls from the shadows. Her hands are held out, away from her clothing. Yeah, she definitely has more weapons stashed in all the fabric.

She watches her brother kick the snot out of the station man and winces.

"Bat, watch them," I say, gesturing to the two idiots on the kitchen floor.

The sister glares when I get close, but she wisely raises her hands when I gesture with my weapon. I search her coat and find another pistol, this one smaller than the one Bat shot out of her hands, and an electric knife similar to the one I have stashed in my ship. I love these things, so it'll be nice to have another. I tuck it into my pocket and stuff the pistol into my pack. She gives me a look I've seen plenty of people give before they try to hit me, but her hands don't so much as twitch. Slight burns ghost her left fingers—the hand holding the gun Bat shot.

Bat's little gun fires. From his hands and knees on the kitchen floor, the brother freezes, withdrawing his hand from Guli's weapon, which he was about to pick up, and glaring at the badger now perched on the kitchen counter. Just a warning shot. Guli is groaning on the floor, holding his stomach, which is just a *little* funny. I've gotta make sure not to be too hard on the brother.

"You." I point at the sister, then at the chair behind her. "Sit. Put these on yourself."

She's giving me the most intense look, as if she's trying to see my face under the hood and past the darkness of the room. My skin crawls. But she does as she's told, catching the cuffs I toss her way.

All things considered, that didn't go too badly. No one's bleeding out a mess I have to clean up, and there aren't *that* many bullet holes in the house. Still, I might have to return after collecting the bounty to give the flustered fisherman some patch-my-house-back-up money. He didn't try to shoot me, so I'm feeling generous.

My okay-with-a-human bar might be in hell.

I toss the brother the other pair of cuffs. He catches them but scrunches his face into a scowl.

"Over there." I point to the chair beside his sister.

He obeys, eyes flickering across the room, looking for something to help him. But he sits, sliding the cuffs on as slowly as possible. The sister is still making intense eye contact. My hood makes it easy to at least *pretend* to ignore her.

"We're done," I tell the fisherman. "Unless Guli here has any more spunk left in him."

The fisherman presses his lips together like he's as annoyed by the man's presence as I am, nudging Guli with his foot.

"Get up, dumbass," he mutters.

Yeah, I'm definitely going to pay to fix their house.

Guli manages to wobble to his feet, looking as if he might puke, and gives me a glare colder than the storm. I take the opportunity to smile and hope the light is sufficient enough for him to see the way the gesture distorts the bottom half of my face. By the way all remnants of color drain from his skin, I'd imagine he sees.

"I take it it's warm enough my ship will start back up?" I ask the fisherman.

He glances at some little box on the wall. Must be a temperature gauge. "Yeah . . . Visibility's probably still bad though."

"He got here." I gesture at Guli with my pistol. He twitches at the glowing weapon.

"Um, his ship is probably logged with the ice pillars out here. You can download the map out of his ship."

Guli glares at the fisherman like he has murder on his mind.

"That would be *lovely,*" I say, making eye contact with the weasel and smiling again.

Something rumbles, the floor trembling, and it takes my brain a second to catch up to the fact it's probably the giant fish rubbing at the underside of the ice again. This time nobody panics.

Then the house shakes so hard I grab the wall behind

me to keep my footing. Bat slides backward into the sink. The fisherman clings to the kitchen counter, both siblings bouncing out of their seats. Guli simply lands back on the floor.

Somewhere in the house, something cracks.

"What the hell did you do?" the fisherman roars.

For half a moment, I think he's yelling at me, but he grabs Guli by his coat and hauls him to his feet. The station man looks more alarmed than when I was pointing my gun at him.

"Did you land out on the ice?"

"Yes, but—"

Another tremor, worse this time. Both men crash to the floor. Something in the wall shakes itself loose, and a glass window shatters, metal shutter popping open. Bat jumps a foot into the air when the ice-filled wind hits him.

"What's going on?" I ask.

"He landed out on the ice field," the fisherman says, grabbing his gun and sprinting for the back room where his wife and children are. "The gengen is ramming the ice; it thinks the ship is in its territory."

I lean out the broken window, ignoring the blast of frigid air and ice crystals in my eyes. A ship half the size of mine is parked on the wide ice field surrounding the house. Cracks spread underneath. Another tremor, and the cracks widen. Chunks of ice rain down from the pillar. The house feels as if it's working itself free of the structure.

Don't land on the ice, the kid at the station warned me. The fish must see the shadow of the ship, which is larger than any one person walking across the ice, even larger than the hovercraft.

It's going to sink this house and our ships right into the ocean.

NINE

There's no way in hell I'm hauling those prisoners onto my ship before this place sinks. They'll put up a fight.

And then there's the parents with their children.

"Bat, watch them!" I call, grabbing Guli by the front of his jacket. "Give me the keylock for your ship."

"What?"

"Keylock! Now!"

He fumbles in his pockets until the little round plate the size of my hand appears. I snatch it, then sprint out the door to the hangar. The cold knocks me back, but I can thank the wind for something: there may be sharp ice flying through the air, but it's blown all the snow off the ice sheet, and it's not very slippery. I bolt for the ship, avoiding cracks in the ice that would probably break even the metal bones in my legs.

A nice thing about being a synthetic monstrosity is I can run really, *really* fast.

I cover the few dozen yards in seconds, trying not to imagine the huge shape getting ready to ram the ice under me at any moment. The ship's gangplank is up, but it isn't a far jump to the airlock. I slide the keylock into its slot, then wait for it to accept and cycle through.

"Come on . . ." I mutter, glancing back at the ice pillar and its house.

Visibility isn't great, even at this distance, but the falling ice is rather obvious.

The airlock clicks open.

And the fish rams into the ice.

If it was bad in the house, I'm fairly surprised I don't break something now. My grip on the ship's railing doesn't save me, and I'm blinking up at the underbelly of the metal craft a moment later, coughing to get breath back into my lungs and trying to scramble to my feet. My hearing aids scream and crackle at all the sudden noise. Jagged edges of the cracked ice dig through my coat and into my human skin, but I grab the ship's leg and haul myself out. My leap back up to the airlock is less graceful this time. My eyes flicker between normal vision and blobs of temperature but begin evening out once I'm on my feet.

Stupid fish.

Slipping inside, I yank the airlock closed and kick the ship back to life. Alarms blare.

<*Unstable ground,*> the ship's computer tells me.

"Gee, thanks."

I'm not even remotely familiar with this model. I've flown plenty of ships, but most were under Audra's instruction, sleek Amerov vessels that were a dream to fly. Even my trash bucket of a ship is more advanced than this thing.

Well, at least it isn't complicated.

Though the outside temperature is returning to a reasonable level, it still takes the engine forever to heat up. It sputters like an old vehicle and refuses to rise more than a foot off the ice.

"Oh, come on, you piece of—"

This time I hear the ice shatter even past the ship's walls. I try not to think about how much it hurts my shoulder when I'm thrown against the metal paneling. The vessel tips to the side. I grab the controls and blast the left thruster before we can flip over like a turtle.

If I die, Bat's going to kill me.

The ship still isn't hovering more than a few feet.

Fine.

Once upright, I hum the engine in the right wing to life, killing the left's power. The ship goes careening out

over the ice field, away from the house, the front weight
of the ship spinning it dangerously. Bringing the thing
to a skidding stop, I stare out the viewport at the mess of
cracked ice a few dozen feet away, listening to the silence.

The main engine is still warming. I can't believe how
long this thing is taking to fly. Fiddling with the port
behind my ear, I try to tap into Bat's frequency over the
storm. It crackles and beeps and generally tries to give
me a headache, but Bat's voice comes over, unclear.

"Aaron?" He sounds concerned.

"I'm fine. Do you think you can get the prisoners into
the ship? I think it might take a while for the engine
to warm up."

"I'll see what I can do."

"Thanks."

I lean back in the captain's chair, feeling the cold now
the adrenaline's wearing off. At least the engine's heating
the ship's cabin. Hopefully Bat can get our vessel back
up and running before the fish decides to give a go at
ramming the ice again now that I've stopped moving. I
try the radar on the control panel, but the thermal map
won't go through all the ice to show me where the fish
is—that or the thing has no heat to it whatsoever. The ice
trembles again, and I lean out the window to attempt to
see the shape of the fish scratching its back along the ice.

Where the ship once was, ice explodes in a flurry of

white. I'm fairly sure I see a giant fin. Water shoots out.

"You've gotta be kidding me . . ."

Right, the sunlight makes them break through the ice. Even in the storm, there's daylight. It's still going to launch itself out. Right next to the pillar of ice that's the family's house.

"Aaron—" Bat's voice crackles back in.

"Working on it!"

Still, the ship only rises a few feet off the ground. Maybe it doesn't even fly higher anymore—it's certainly old enough. And no guns. I check behind me for any weapon compartment. Nothing but the small cramped space I'm in.

What kind of ship doesn't have guns?

I take back all my ideas about this bounty hunt going well.

Firing the wings back to life, I shoot the stupid little trash ship out across the ice, back toward the house. This thing doesn't have much control, and I spin it around, bumping hard into the side of the pillar to bring it to a stop. Cracks have spread all the way to the house. I almost land in one as I jump from the airlock. My ship is still cold and asleep—Bat's probably having a hell of a time keeping the prisoners in check now that everything's gone chaotic. At least my airlock opens to the sound of my voice. I fire up the engines, wanting to cheer when they burst to life. Another tremor. Picking myself up off the floor, I back the ship out of the hangar as fast as possible without breaking a wing. I hope the house will hold up to the weight of the ice it's built into.

Bat's still in there.

"All right, you big ugly fish," I mutter, spinning the ship into the air and bringing the guns to life. I didn't originally have such large weapons on this thing. The first big bounty I ever chased bought me this ship. The second bought me the heavy-duty firepower, which is enough to take down most Amerov vessels.

Below, I see the little hovercraft zipping out after me. *What in the world is he thinking?*

Sure, he does this for a living, but he's going to get himself killed. The vehicle has a tiny gun. Bright lights flare as he zips in a circle around all the fracturing ice.

Oh. I know what he's doing. Smart guy. As long as he gets out of the way afterward.

I get a good look at the fish as it finally flings its massive body into daylight. It's much like an eel, skin a grayish green, massive fins feathering the sides of its long face. Even from my height, I glimpse all the teeth and shudder. The creature launches itself farther out, annoyed by the fisherman's shots and attempting to flop out and snatch him.

Giving me a really nice target now that it's vulnerable.

Swooping low and tipping the ship directly down so I have a perfect view out the front viewport, I fire. The fisherman zips the hell out of the way, out over the ice and toward a nearby pillar, so I'm free to go wild on this thing. The first few shots only seem to annoy it. It tries to flop up and toward my ship, jaws gaping, but I yank the ship up with plenty of time.

"Sorry, but you tried to kill me," I mutter, aiming at the soft underside of its jaw.

It lands on the ice and doesn't move.

Leaning over the controls, I watch the fisherman speed over, parking a little too near it for my comfort.

"Bat?" I ask, tapping on the port behind my ear. "You good?"

No answer. *Stupid comms.*

I steer the ship down along the ice, landing near the house but not inside the hangar. It doesn't look very stable anymore. From out on the ice, the fisherman waves cheerfully. Without bothering with the gangplank, I swing down from the airlock.

A blast of heat hits right above my ear.

TEN

The bullet tears open the edge of my ship's wing but doesn't give me more than a slight burn. I dive behind the landing gear, peeking around the edge at whatever idiot decided to take a clear shot and actually *miss*.

Guli pauses in the wide frame of the hangar door and blinks at me.

There's gratitude for you. Saved his ass *and* his unhelpful ship and he *still* tries to shoot me.

This is why I keep the hell away from humans.

Grumbling, I pull my other pistol—the one I'd been using was dropped somewhere in the chaos, probably on the kitchen floor. Guli's mouth pops open, and he sprints behind the fugitive's ship. I sigh. Probably could've taken a shot at him. I was hoping to get out of this day without murdering anyone. Even slimy weasels.

"Bat." I fiddle with my comm again. It gives me static and not much else. "Bat, what are you doing in there? I think the station idiot picked up one of the fugitives' guns."

The one he fired was definitely heavy-duty. Still no answer from Bat. The vaguest worry begins in my chest. These comms are unreliable as hell, but I'd think the little critter would've made an appearance by now.

Jumping to the airlock will put me right out in the open, not to mention the time it would take to cycle open. I glance over my shoulder at the fisherman, but he doesn't appear to notice the new development. Stars only know what he's doing with that fish. Sliding under the belly of my ship, I climb up the back and over the hull, peeking down. From here, I catch Guli crouching behind the wing of the fugitive's ship, trying to get an eye on me. Carefully, I aim above his head and fire, trying not to smile when he nearly jumps out of his skin.

"Move out, idiot," I call.

He tries to duck farther under the ship, and I fire at his feet. I can *feel* his glare even from up here. I wiggle my fingers in a wave.

He shuffles out from behind the ship, gun still in his hand but both of them raised.

I slide down the ship and snatch the pistol. This close, he cowers from me. I don't have another set of cuffs, but there are ropes among the stacked tarps in the corner of the hangar.

It's quite satisfying seeing him tied up, glaring at the icy ground.

Walking him in front of me, I push past the heavy door into the house. Lights are on now, illuminating the room and offering a better look at everyone's faces. I'm glad they can't see me. The mother has appeared from the back room—the kids are nowhere to be seen—and is aiming her own rifle at the two convicts in their chairs.

"Bat?" I call.

Guli decides struggling is his best bet, gesturing at the mother as if she's supposed to help him. The look she gives him is nervous but unimpressed.

"Sit down," I say, trying to shove him to the floor. He doesn't get a chair like a dignified person.

"I'm going to file a complaint!" he snaps, still trying to keep his feet. "Amerov numbers aren't allowed to assault citizens—"

A laugh bubbles up in my chest. "Yeah, we've been over this. *Sit.*"

He flails like that giant fish trying to flop out of the ice. I kick the inside of his thigh—not hard enough to break anything, but hopefully he'll lose feeling for a minute or two. He yanks on my coat but lands hard on his ass anyway, flailing back and scooting away from me with a yelp.

Warmth from the house slides over my face and ears and through my hair—all the places the hood was covering.

I get a good look at the terror on the woman's face before she fires.

This one's a much closer shot, grazing my skin. Fire explodes along my shoulder, dulled by adrenaline. Guli yelps, nearly face-planting on the kitchen floor when I shove him farther away as I duck. My gun is raised in a second, but I don't want to shoot her. Hell, she just looks scared. Her children are in the other room, her home was nearly destroyed, and I know what I look like and all the rumors that come with rogue cyborgs—

I slide out of the way as she fires again, one of the cabinets exploding. I aim for her rifle but don't need to. Bat comes flying up from somewhere, latching his sharp jaws around her arm. I don't know where his gun went, but one of his metal legs looks limp and lifeless.

Someone shot at him.

I'm willing to bet it was her. Maybe I should've taken my shot. Bat wouldn't have attacked for no reason.

She shrieks, rifle flying, trying to shake him. Which isn't going to work. Kicking her gun aside, I shove her to the ground and grab Bat by the scruff of the neck.

"Let her go. I'm fine!"

He flails his legs as I tug him off, but he unlocks his jaw. I tuck him under my arm and keep him there.

"Stop screaming. I wasn't going to hurt you!" I snap.

She doesn't stop, scooting away and throwing a piece of debris at me that bounces off my temple. Her arm is bleeding. From the corner of the room, the children join in. I don't bother to look at them. My hearing aids crackle.

For heaven's sake.

"*Shut up!*" I yell as loud as my lungs will go.

Everything falls so silent my head hurts.

"Don't even think about it!" I snap at the brother, who's using the distraction to wriggle his way toward one of the weapons. He freezes and scowls. Grabbing each of the discarded guns, I toss them into the sink, tucking the pistol I lost back into my belt. I fling a kitchen towel at the mother.

"Wrap your arm in that and try not to shoot at people who weren't planning on hurting you."

She doesn't look even a hint calmer but does as she's told, then scrambles to her feet and shuffles to her children, putting herself between them and me. They peer at me around her legs, and I try not to think about their expressions twisted in fear. My face feels hot, and I wish it were from adrenaline and not shame.

I really should be used to this by now.

Out the busted window, I can see the fisherman heading back on his little hovercraft. *Well, this won't be fun.*

Waving my pistol at the siblings, I point them toward the door. "Walk."

They do not.

"Ya know, if you two were half as smart as you'd have to be to break out of Clock, you'd know to listen to the cyborg with a gun and his friend who will happily bite you if I ask him to."

Both get to their feet. The brother's eyes are still flickering about as he scrambles for a way to get out of this. The sister looks less concerned about scheming and more concerned about staring at me. If she hadn't been giving me this weird look even before my hood was pulled down, I'd think it was my appearance. I make direct eye contact, scowling, which usually puts most people off gawking. Her eyebrows pull together, but she doesn't look away, even when she bumps into the open doorframe as I herd them out.

Weird lady.

Behind me, the mother has the good sense to let us leave and not make a dive for the weapons in the sink. Guli scoots farther away as I pass.

Leaning over him, I say, "Don't follow me. I dislike

having to shoot idiots."

To his credit, he at least tries to scowl instead of only looking mortified.

"Is everything all right?" the fisherman asks as I shove the siblings toward my ship with the muzzle of my gun. Then he sees my face and does a bit of a half jump backward. I should've pulled my hood back up.

"Your wife hurt her arm, but she's fine," I say, which doesn't sound too much like a lie.

With rather obvious concern, he glances at the house, then at the siblings. He doesn't appear too thrilled about the whole situation. "Er . . . what about their ship?"

"Keep it. You're going to need money for repairs."

"That's *our ship*." The brother tries to turn on me, but I give him a good shove on the ice. "We have personal things in there! Let us get them!"

"You're both going to Clock," I say. "Where exactly do you think you're going to keep these personal things?"

Both are quiet, the brother glancing at their ship under the tarps, the sister still staring with all that intensity. A small annoying part of me feels guilty. My ship is my home—I'd never abandon it. But I'm also not wrong. Anything I let them take will only be stripped and discarded once Clock gets their hands on them.

My airlock cycles open, and I set Bat inside so he can activate the gangplank. The brother is scowling, so I do the same. Still staring, the sister leans over and tugs on his sleeve until he leans down. She whispers something into his ear. I don't particularly care what they're trying to plot, not with them both cuffed and free of weapons, but I lean against the massive gun under my ship's wing just to be dramatic.

The brother's face goes completely blank. His eyes flicker over me as if he's realized something, and now they're both staring as if they've seen a ghost.

These two are missing a few marbles.

Once the gangplank unfolds, I gesture at them to get inside.

"What's your name?" the brother asks, which is the last thing I thought he'd ask.

"Guy who's going to shoot you if you don't walk up that gangplank."

The sister presses her lips together.

Over the tops of their heads, I see the fisherman stomping back out of his house. Wonderful. I really don't want to shoot him either.

"Get in the ship," I mutter.

Both see the fisherman and, to my surprise, head for the gangplank. From across the ice, the man looks to be raising his rifle. I'm certain his wife told him Bat attacked her. And probably left out the part where she tried to shoot me for no damn reason.

I raise my own weapon. "Don't do it. Don't even think about doing it."

He stops, face scrunched in a scowl, ice building back up in his beard.

From inside, Bat's panicked voice calls, "Aaron, under the ship!"

ELEVEN

I jump, catching myself blindly on the wing of the ship, nearly slipping off, right in time for a bullet to blaze sharply by where I was standing.

Both siblings scatter.

In opposite directions.

Sighing, I lean over the wing and aim at the woman currently sprinting toward Guli's ship abandoned on the ice. The bounty is only good if they're alive, but shooting them both in the leg will make all this much easier. So what if I have to clean some blood off the floors of my ship? Plus, if I only manage to get one, I want her. She was the one caught on Amerov and who later broke out of Clock—her individual reward is higher than his.

I squeeze off a shot, but the ice and wind are throwing

off my sight, not to mention the wild blobs of blue and red my eyes are giving me over everything else. She has the good sense to bob and weave as she runs.

From under my ship, there's another shot. The fisherman is still where he stopped near the house, looking confused, which means someone untied Guli. The stupid woman probably, or perhaps even the fisherman himself. If Guli fires into the wing turbines, I'll never get off this planet.

This really isn't my day.

"Bat!" I call. "Get her. Alive."

The guns on the ship are too large to use on a person without killing them—I see Bat scrambling to the top of the hull on three working legs, his little gun clamped between his jaws. He must have found it in all the chaos. Sliding down the wing, I attempt to get a look under the belly of the ship without sticking my head out like a giant ugly target.

Yep, it's Guli. He's prodding at the metal plating under the ship with his pistol, probably trying to find a vulnerable spot a handgun will fire through. There aren't many, not on a vessel like this meant to take battle damage, but with today's luck, I'm not taking chances. I fire at his feet and get the slimmest satisfaction at the way he yelps, scrambling off along the ice at top speed, heading for the opposite side of the ship. Hauling myself upright, I crawl over the hull, past Bat, and slide onto the other wing in time to see him scramble out. He turns and aims under the ship as if he's still expecting me to be there. He's given me enough of a headache, so I aim for his kneecap and hope the injury will bother him for the rest of his life.

He doesn't scream and manages to keep ahold of his gun when he falls. Sliding to the ice, I raise my weapon, stalking toward him.

"Drop it or the next one puts you out forever."

"Freak," he spits.

It's hilarious he thinks I care. "Yep, you're right. Drop it."

He glares, and then his eyes flicker to the top of the ship, where I hear Bat trying to take down the fleeing woman.

"Don't—" I warn.

He flings his arm upward, gun aimed.

When I fire, he falls still.

Dropping my pistol to my side, I stare and sigh, turning my back on the sight.

What did he think would happen, taking aim at my best friend?

"Aaron," Bat's voice crackles on the comm. "Get in the ship. I couldn't get her."

"Coming."

I sprint under the belly as the engine roars to life.

Out across the ice, I see her trying to get Guli's ship off the ground. She doesn't appear to be having a good go of it, but that'll make it easier to shoot the thrusters out and bring her down.

Who knows where the brother ran off to.

The fisherman has crept near the ship, jumping when I appear from underneath. His rifle is half-raised, but he doesn't look like he'll take a shot at me. I make a "move" gesture with my pistol even though he isn't in my way—I don't want him getting any ideas.

"We're leaving. Go back to your house and wait."

The gangplank is already pulled up with the engines starting.

"Aaron, come on!"

"Yeah, yeah."

I grab the ladder along the side of the airlock and pull myself up as the ship rises. Getting in through the top hatch will be easier anyway, and that little planet jumper of a ship won't be able to outrun this one, let alone stand up to even a bit of firepower—

There's the ear-splitting noise of an old gun going off, and my already-bleeding shoulder explodes with pain.

TWELVE

My hand loses its grip on the ladder. It isn't far of a drop, a dozen feet, but it knocks the wind out of me, and my gun clatters along the ice.

Swearing, I roll over in time for the next shot to miss.

I guess the fisherman didn't appreciate his wife's arm getting chewed.

I push myself up, ignoring the fire in my shoulder, glaring while Bat spins the ship back around. Dodging bullets unarmed wasn't something I wanted to add to the list of things to do today.

The fisherman looks panicked the shot didn't faze me much, eyes wide as he fumbles to raise the rifle.

The huge blinding blue heat flare of a ship's guns sparks a line in front of him. My eyes flash white, sending a pounding headache into my temples. The fisherman falls, scrambling away. The fugitive's ship zips between the two of us, no longer covered in tarps, blocking him from sight, the bottom thrusters sending ice and freezing air buffeting me back.

I get a good look at the brother through the glass roof of his ship as he waves at me to get back into my own craft.

Did he just . . . ?

Save my life?

Grabbing my gun, I yank myself up beside the airlock with my good arm, climb onto the hull of the ship, and drop through the top hatch. The brother shoots off into the atmosphere. So does the sister in Guli's stolen vessel.

Well, I guess that thing *can* get airborne.

"Damn," I mumble, sealing the hatch.

"Aaron—"

"I'm fine. Let's get off this icicle."

Bat follows them up. Visibility is still terrible, but straight up through the clouds isn't too difficult. As we break the clouds, the planet's red star reappears. I rest my forehead in my hand. My shoulder throbs even if the sudden headache is easing. The burning trembling of the ship as we leave the planet doesn't help.

I hate this bounty job.

"I'm going to fix my shoulder," I say, heading toward

my bunk room and the connected washroom. I can tell the old-fashioned bullet didn't hit anything vital, and I don't bleed much. My body clots injuries in a matter of seconds. As long as there isn't anything metal to repair, the flesh will heal up fine in a week or less.

"They're splitting off," Bat says as we break out into empty space.

"What?"

He points his limp leg at the console. I need to fix that—it doesn't look terribly damaged, probably a wire or some little part I can repair with the components I have here on our ship. Hopefully. I wouldn't even know where to get new ones.

Joining him, I watch the heat signals of the ships as they break off, each heading in its own direction. There aren't many planets out here, but a few small ones dot the vastness of space where they might attempt to hide. I need to pick one, at least for now. I can deliver one before going after the other. A job this big is worth the extra time and effort.

And I know who's more valuable. And who has a worse ship, which'll be easier to track and chase.

"We're following her?" Bat asks.

"Yeah," I say. "We're following her."

THANK YOU!

Thank you so much for reading *In Dying Starlight*! Leaving a review on Amazon, Goodreads, or any other platform you prefer helps support this book and reach new readers!

To follow along with more of Emily McCosh's works, you can sign up for her author newsletter at *oceansinthesky. com* to be the first to learn about new releases, artwork, unreleased content, sneak peeks at the next novellas, and any other nerdy book news.

ABOUT THE
AUTHOR

Emily McCosh is a graphic designer and writer of strange things. She currently lives in California with her two parents, two dogs, one tree swing, and innumerable characters who need to learn some manners. Her short fiction has appeared in *Beneath Ceaseless Skies*, *Shimmer Magazine*, *Galaxy's Edge*, *Flash Fiction Online*, *Nature: Futures*, and elsewhere.

Under the Earth, Over the Sky, her debut novel, is forthcoming in November of 2022 after a successful Kickstarter, and her short story collection, *All the Woods She Watches Over: Stories & Poetry*, and was a finalist for the Next Generation Indie Book Awards.

Find her online on her writing YouTube channel and TikTok full of wild writing skits and bookish content.

Website: oceansinthesky.com

YouTube: Emily McCosh

TikTok: emilymccosh

Instagram: emily_mccosh

Facebook & Twitter: @wordweaveremily

Printed in the USA
CPSIA information can be obtained
at www.ICGtesting.com
LVRC092246251124
797615LV00001B/1